This book

belongs to

....

2021 Sage's Tower Publishing

Copyright © 2021 by Sarah Atherton

Cover Design and Illustrations © 2021 by Chrish Vindhy

Published in the United States by Sage's Tower Publishing.

Sage's Tower Publishing is a registered trademark.

Hardcover ISBN: 978-1-63706-018-6
Softcover ISBN: 978-1-63706-017-9
EPUB ISBN: 978-1-63706-019-3

Printed in the United States of America

www.sagestowerpublishing.com

Bella's Butterflies

Written by
Sarah Atherton

Illustrated by.
Chrish Vindhy

For my family near and far.

-SA-

Bella didn't want to go to school. She had a strange fluttering feeling in her tummy.

"Are you OK?"
asked Miss Lindsay when
she saw Bella looking sad.

Bella wasn't OK. She was worried.
And when she worried, her tummy
felt all twisty and swirly.

"I don't want to do the math test.
It's too hard!" complained Bella.

"Ah, I see," said her teacher.
"You have butterflies in your tummy."

Bella had never heard anything
so silly in her life!
She doubted very much there
were butterflies in her tummy.
She knew butterflies came from
caterpillars and she didn't
remember swallowing any of those.

At play time, Bella's friends could tell she was upset.

"What's wrong?" asked Ned.

"Miss Lindsay said I've got butterflies in my tummy," answered Bella.

"Let me see," said Clarissa.
Bella opened her mouth wide.

"Nope, I can't see anything," said Clarissa.

"I need to let them out," said Bella.
"My tummy feels horrid."

"Why don't you do a handstand?"
suggested Ned.
"That way, they might fall out."

Bella did the longest, straightest
handstand she could manage.

She stayed like that
until her face turned bright red,
but it was no good -
the butterflies stayed put.

"Try jumping up and down," said Clarissa. "That might make them fly out."

Bella jumped…and jumped… and jumped.

Ned and Clarissa joined in to see who could jump the highest. It was fun but,

FLUTTER!

She could still feel the butterflies.

"That didn't work," said Bella, feeling hot and sweaty.

"I've got another idea," said Ned.
"I wonder if butterflies are ticklish?"

And with that, Ned and Clarissa tickled
Bella until she was laughing and giggling,
rolling and wriggling.

The three of them lay on the grass
and gazed at the sky. Bella had forgotten
all about the butterflies.

And then the bell rang.
"Oh no! Time for math," groaned Bella.

In the classroom, Bella looked at her math problems and felt the butterflies fluttering and flapping, twisting and turning inside her tummy.
She tried the first one, but it was too hard.

"Miss Lindsay, the butterflies won't keep still in my tummy," said Bella.

"Why don't you try taking some deep breaths?" suggested Miss Lindsay.
"Butterflies love fresh air."
Bella breathed in…and out…in…and out…

She tried the next question…still too hard.
The butterflies were flapping like mad!

This was no good.
Bella felt like crying.
She looked at Ned. He was
working through his test very quickly.

She glanced at Clarissa, who also had her
head down, working hard.

Then Bella thought about her friends and
how they had tried to help her get rid of
her butterflies.

She smiled as she remembered how they had jumped as high as they could. The butterflies calmed their wings once again and Bella was able to concentrate on her work for a while.

When she got to the second question, the fluttery feeling returned to her tummy.

But Bella had another funny memory of how she and her friends had
giggled while lying on the grass and she couldn't feel the butterflies anymore.

Bella worked her way through the rest
of her test and smiled at her friends.
Miss Lindsay called out the answers,
and to her surprise,

Bella scored higher than
she ever had before in math.
She was grinning
with delight.

Bella knew she had found a brilliant
way to get rid of the butterflies
if they ever came back.
All she needed was a little bit
of help from her friends.

For now, Bella was happy to see the
butterflies fluttering around outside.

The End

CPSIA information can be obtained
at www.ICGtesting.com
Printed in the USA
BVHW020918170621
609820BV00002B/5